D0114530

Creative Director: Susie Garland Rice
Design: Colston Rife

Dalmatian Press owns all art and editorial material.
ISBN: 1-57759-259-X
© 1999 Dalmatian Press. All rights reserved.
Printed and bound in the U.S.A. The DALMATIAN PRESS name,
logo and spotted spine are trademarks of Dalmatian Press, Franklin, Tennessee 37067.

10744a/tort&hare

# THE TORTOISE & THE HARE

An ÆSOP Fable
**adapted by tess fries**
**illustrated by danny brooks dalby**

Dalmatian Press ®

One fine day

in a clearing by the brook,

next to oak trees towering high,

A hare told his friends

just how fast he was—

seems he could almost fly!

"I've never been beaten!"

claimed the hare with a grin.

All the animals listened in wonder.

I've raced dogs down the road

and a fox through the glen,

why, I've even out-distanced a hunter!"

"I'm faster than you—every one!"

bragged the hare,

as the whiskers just twitched on his face.

And then with a hop

he cried to the crowd,

"I challenge you all to a race!"

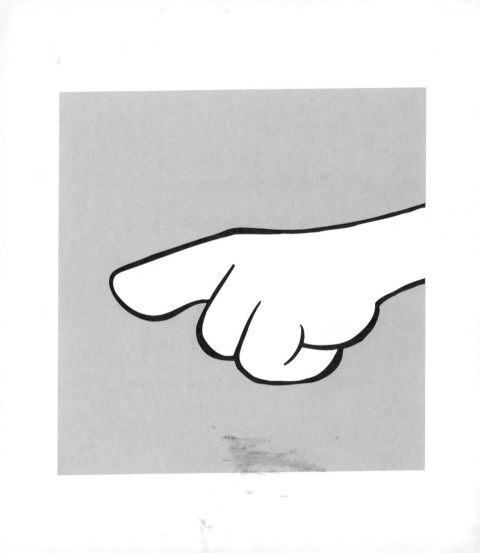

The skunk crept away,

and the bears looked scared.

The opossum shuffled his feet.

But a clear small voice

from in the crowd asked,

"When and where shall we meet?"

Who could have said that?

They all had to know,

when the tortoise said loud and clear,

"I take your challenge,

my fine Mr. Hare,"

And his friends all started to cheer!

"Why, this must be a joke!"

said the hare with a laugh.

"Beating you won't even be fair!"

"Don't boast till you've won,"

said our wise tortoise friend.

"Shall we race right now, Mr. Hare?"

The course was set

and the runners took their mark.

Soon the hare was clear out of sight.

The tortoise inched ahead

through the heat of the day

trying with all of his might.

The hare looked around.

He was miles up ahead,

and he chuckled while mopping his brow.

"I'll just rest right here

with a nice little nap.

I know that I'll win anyhow!"

Inch by inch, slow and safe

the tortoise went along

over sticks and stones and holes.

He never gave up

and he never looked back.

He just kept his sights on his goals.

The hare yawned and stretched,

and blinked his little eyes,

as he woke to the sun going down.

He leapt to his feet

and he looked down the road,

but the tortoise was nowhere around.

Then the hare heard cheering

from the crowd up ahead.

Why, that tortoise had practically won!

So the hare dashed forward

on past the finish line,

but the tortoise was already done!

"You're so very fast,"

said the tortoise to the hare,

"I surely can't keep up your pace.

I go steady and slow,

with my eyes on my goal,

and I win almost every race."